A GOOD SECRET

written by Julie Carter

illustrated by Kevin Banal

A GOOD SECRET

written by Julie Carter

illustrated by Kevin Banal

This book was written for the very special boys and girls who have good secrets to share. With family anything is possible!

Dedicated to my kids and husband who bring me lots of joy, humility, and strength! Love you!

- Mom

edited by: Amora Carter & Christian Carter

Mommy's having a baby, but she says it's a secret.
SHHHHH!!!!

Daddy says we can't tell just yet so we have to keep it.
SHHHHH!!

What a big secret to keep for such a busy mouth like mine.

My sister, she can keep a secret just fine.

We can't help but wonder who the baby will look like this time.

My sister and me look like daddy, so maybe this time the baby will look like mommy.

We watch mommy's belly grow bigger and bigger and tying her shoelaces has become harder.

Getting in and out the car is funny to see.

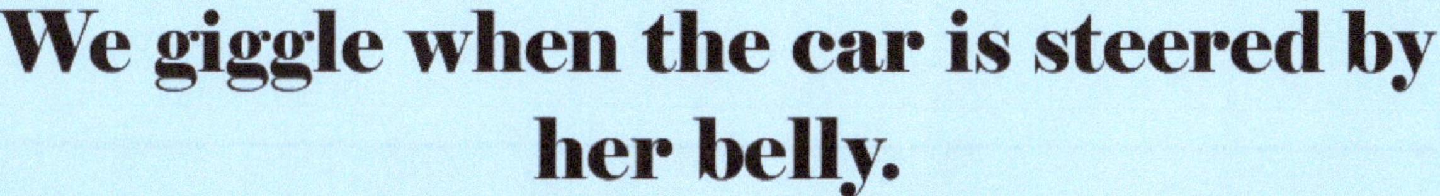
We giggle when the car is steered by her belly.

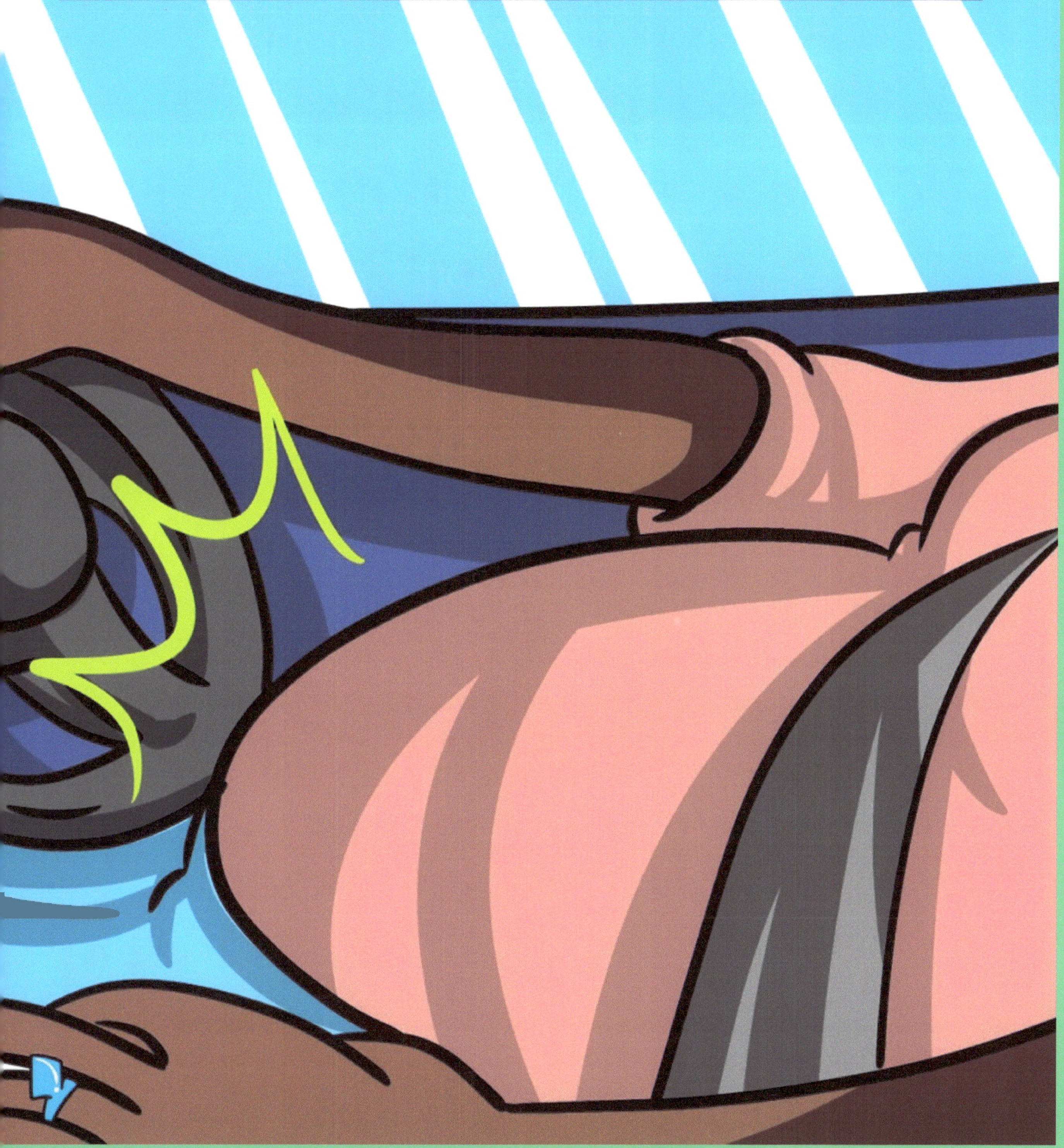

Soon mommy's belly just can't grow anymore.

Guess What?!

We don't have to keep the secret any more.

One evening my sister and me head to bed, but Grandma tucks us in instead.

Mommy and Daddy video chat the next morning and they're grinning.

Before the conversation begins,
mommy and daddy shout...

Surprise! It's twins!

My sister and me are surprised and delighted to see features of our mother in our new brother and sister!

There's two?! Who knew?

We thought we were keeping a secret from the world, but mommy and daddy kept a secret that they were having a boy and a girl!

Now a family of six.

We look forward to even more love and fun-filled family trips!

THE END!

www.ingramcontent.com/pod-product-compliance
Lightning Source LLC
Chambersburg PA
CBHW041637110726
48005CB00002B/626